Hi, Parents!

Your child's love of reading starts here, with HarperAlley's **I Can Read Comics!**

HARPER alley

I Can Read Comics introduces children to the world of graphic novel storytelling and encourages visual literacy in emerging readers. Comics inspire reader engagement unlike any other format. They ask readers to infer and answer questions, like:

1. What do I read first? Image or text?
2. Why is this word balloon shaped this way, and that word balloon shaped that way?
3. Why is a character making that facial expression? Are they happy, angry, excited, sad?

From the comics your child reads with you to the first comic they read on their own, there are **I Can Read Comics** for every stage of reading:

LEVEL 1
Simple stories for shared reading.

LEVEL 2
Engaging stories for children reading on their own.

LEVEL 3
Complex stories for independent readers.

The magic of graphic novel storytelling lies between the gutters.
Unlock the magic with…

I Can Read Comics!

Visit **ICanRead.com** for information on enriching your child's reading experience.

I Can Read *Comics* Cartooning Basics

Panel
A moment in time

Gutter
The space between panels

Tier
One row of panels

Word Balloons When someone talks, thinks, whispers, or screams, their words go in here:

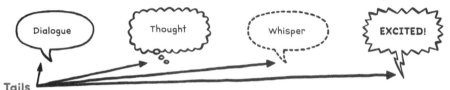

Dialogue

Thought

Whisper

EXCITED!

Tails
Point to whoever is talking / thinking / whispering / screaming / etc.

A quick how-to-read comics guide:

In a **panel**, read the text on the **left** first.

Then, read the text on the **right**.

Remember to...

Read the text along with the image, paying close attention to the character's acting, the action, and/or the scene. Every little detail matters!

No dialogue? No problem!

If there is no dialogue within a panel, take the time to read the image. Visual cues are just as important as text, so don't forget about them!

On a page, **start here**, in the **top left** corner!

After that, read the panel immediately to the **right**.

When you're done up there, come down here and read **this** panel **next**!

ME NEXT! ME NEXT!

You're almost there...

YOU MADE IT! You just read a comic page!

YAY!

For my mom and dad —S.W.

HarperAlley is an imprint of HarperCollins Publishers.
I Can Read® and I Can Read Book® are trademarks of HarperCollins Publishers.

Tiny Tales: Shell Quest
Copyright © 2021 by Steph Waldo
All rights reserved. Printed in the United States of America.
No part of this book may be used or reproduced in any manner whatsoever without written permission except in the case of brief quotations embodied in critical articles and reviews. For information address HarperCollins Children's Books, a division of HarperCollins Publishers, 195 Broadway, New York, NY 10007.
www.icanread.com

Library of Congress Control Number: 2021933199
ISBN 978-0-06-306783-7 (trade bdg.) — ISBN 978-0-06-306782-0 (pbk.)

Book design by Joe Merkel
21 22 23 24 25 LSCC 10 9 8 7 6 5 4 3 2 1 ❖ First Edition

TiNY TALeS

SHELL QUEST

by Steph Waldo

HARPER alley

An Imprint of HarperCollinsPublishers

scoot
scoot

POP!

My shell!

Oh, no!

Don't worry, I'll find another one!

We hope so.

Come back when you do!

A NATURE GUIDE
SLUG vs SNAIL

- Land slugs grow up to 10 inches (25.4cm).

- Slugs have no visible shell and live under loose bark, stones, and logs.

- Most slugs live up to 6 years in the wild.

- Land snails vary greatly in size, from under an inch up to 12 inches or more.

- Snails have shells on their backs.

- Most land snails live 2 to 3 years in the wild, but some can live more than 10.

Both are called **gastropods**, which comes from the Greek word **gastros**, meaning **stomach**, and **podos**, meaning **foot**.

For more information on slugs and snails, check out: kids.nationalgeographic.com, kids.britannica.com, and carnegiemnh.org.

"stomach foot"